JUVE C

JUVE C

CRANE BOY

WRITTEN BY
DIANA COHN

ILLUSTRATED BY
YOUME

Every October, I wait for the black-necked cranes to return. The birds fly over the highest mountains in the world to winter in the soft wet fields of the Phobjika Valley where I live. Here they grow fat, eating worms, slugs and the fallen grains from the buckwheat we harvest each year.

I want to be the first
to see the cranes.

I look out my classroom window and shout, "Look, the cranes!"

My teacher sighs. "Kinga, that's only a flock of crows!"

Another day I see black specks in the sky. "The cranes!"

My friend Pema laughs and says, "They're pigeons, Kinga!"

Day after day, I wait for the birds we call *trung trung* with their long necks and their loud squawking calls.

"They're here!" I shout.

Pema says, "Yes. I see them too!" Everyone runs to the windows.

The cranes circle the golden roof of the monastery where monks chant prayers for the well-being of all living things.

They fly over the Crane
Center where Kado works. He
is called the Caretaker of the Cranes.
Kado tells us about these birds that have visited
Bhutan for thousands of years.

"Long ago many more cranes came to our valley, but
this year we counted only 203," he says. His eyes are sad. "But
the more we learn to care for them, the more we can help their
numbers grow.

"To protect the cranes, we preserve our wetlands so they
have enough to eat," Kado says, "but we need to find more ways
to help them, for they are our sisters and brothers."

What can I do to help?

That night I tell my family about Kado and the cranes.

Grandmother says, "*Trung trung* bring us good luck for our crops."

"For hundreds of years," Mother says, "artists have painted them on the walls of our houses and monasteries."

Father finishes his butter tea and says, "The cranes bring strength to those who love archery."

I want to be a great archer like my father. At the village archery contest, he pulls back his bow until just the right moment, then lets the string go. *Zing!* When his arrow hits the target over 400 feet away, his team celebrates with a dance. They each stand on one leg, then turn and jump up and down, just like the cranes.

"Wah-ha!" they sing, thanking the cranes that have flown so far to bring the archers strength and good luck.

Maybe there is a way I can help the cranes.

The next day, I ask my class, "If people come to our archery contests and to our festivals to see the monks dance, would they also come to a festival to see us dance for the cranes?" Their faces shine, *yes!* Our teacher says, "We must ask the monks for permission because all festivals are held in their courtyards."

"Kuzu-zangpo la," we say, greeting the monks. "Can you help us make a new festival with a dance for the cranes?"

A monk named Sangay says, "Our dances have been performed the same way for centuries and each one takes hours of practice."

He sees our disappointment and his face slowly breaks into a smile. "Dancing to tell stories is part of our tradition," he says, "but before we can help you make a crane dance, you must first watch the birds and learn from them."

We watch a crane standing on one leg, holding as still as a day with no wind. When I try to balance on one leg, I wobble and fall down.

A crane throws back her head with her beak to the sun. Her black head has a spot of orange-red, the same color as the polished coral bead my mother wears around her neck to keep her safe.

When the cranes bow down, jump up and flap their wings, I do the same.

What if I had wings?

Pema laughs and joins me, flapping her arms.

"Pema," I say, "the cranes are almost as tall as we are!"

When we show the monks our crane movements, Sangay says, "You are now ready to learn some dance secrets."

The monks show us how to turn and spin on one leg and then the other. It's hard! I get so dizzy I have to sit down. Every day we practice.

One afternoon, Sangay says, "We sent invitations for the Crane Festival to every village in Bhutan."

The morning of the festival,
hundreds of people come
in their finest clothes.
The monks appear first in brilliant
yellow silk costumes with animal
masks on their heads. They dance
barefoot, leaping, swirling
and beating their drums.

Now it is our turn. When the cymbals sound, we walk to the center of the courtyard. *What if I get dizzy and fall? What if I turn the wrong way and bump into Pema? I'm afraid I'll let everyone down.* I listen to the music and wave my arms like wings, up and down. I throw my head back and look up at the sky. *I imagine flying.* I balance on one leg, then spin in a circle with all the other dancers, turning and turning until...

...I spiral up and up, lifted by the same air currents that lift the cranes. I swirl higher and higher into the air until I float down to feel the ground beneath me.

After the dances are over, we are surrounded by family and friends.

Mother says, "Kinga, I will call you Crane Boy!"

Kado says, "*Trung trung* are your true sisters and brothers."

Then the guest of honor, the King of Bhutan, says, "You have given our country a new festival. From now on, we will honor the cranes with your dances."

When the days grow warm, the cranes return to their summer home in Tibet. There they will build their nests, lay their eggs and have their babies. I chant prayers for their well-being as I watch them fly away until they are just little black specks in the sky.

Months will pass before I see the cranes again. I will be taller. When they return, I'll help Kado count them. *I know there will be more.* Until then I will practice turning and spinning so I can dance for them at the next Festival of the Cranes.

"I believe that any real and lasting solution to
global issues can only come through a universal wave of
human empathy, desire and passion for the common good."

–*King Jigme Khesar Namgyel Wangchuck*

"The world grows smaller and smaller, more and more
interdependent. Today more than ever before, life must
be characterized by a sense of Universal Responsibility,
not only nation to nation and human to human,
but also human to other forms of life."

–*His Holiness the XIV Dalai Lama*

A NOTE FROM DIANA & YOUME

Crane Boy could not have been created without the kindness and open-heartedness of the people we met in Bhutan who introduced us to their world. Guide Kesang Dorji shared his knowledge of Bhutanese history and culture. Teachers and students invited us to watch them practice dances for the Crane Festival. We were welcomed to visit them in their classrooms and in their homes. The dustjacket and some pages of *Crane Boy* include drawings of cranes by students from the Bayta Elementary School in the Phobjika Valley.

We also met with scientists, environmentalists and economists working to protect the habitats where cranes can thrive alongside humans.

We offer this book in gratitude to the people of Bhutan and to the sacred heavenly cranes who have touched the human imagination for thousands of years with their grace, beauty and majesty.

BHUTAN

Bhutan is a tiny country in South Asia, sandwiched between two large and powerful countries—China (and the Tibetan Plateau) to the north and India to the south. Bhutan lies in the Himalaya Mountains with a population of less than 800,000 people.

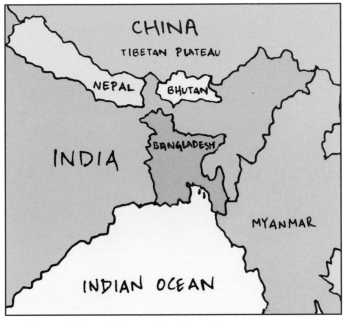

Dzongkha is Bhutan's official language. Although there are at least 19 dialects and languages spoken throughout the country, the English language is spoken in all schools.

Archery is the national sport in Bhutan.

The Bhutanese dress in traditional clothing. Men and boys wear a knee-length robe in different colors and patterns called a *gho*. Women and girls wear ankle-length dresses in beautiful silk or cotton called a *kira*.

Some unusual mammals live in Bhutan, including tigers, snow leopards, yak, red panda, and golden langur monkeys. Under Bhutanese law, 60% of the country will remain forested for all time, protecting plants, animals and birds.

THE PHOBJIKA VALLEY

Many families who live in the Phobjika Valley are farmers who grow potatoes and raise cattle, horses and sheep. The growing demand for these potatoes has encouraged farmers to convert wetlands into more farms. These wetlands, however, are the precious habitat for the black-necked cranes. Organizations like the Royal Society for the Protection of Nature (RSPN) and local village leaders encourage farmers to either preserve the wetlands or to grow their crops organically, free of pesticides, so the cranes can eat healthy non-toxic food during their winter months in the Valley.

In Bhutan, black-necked cranes are called *trung trung* and are celebrated in songs, paintings, poetry, and of course, in dance. All over the world, cranes are symbols of happiness, loyalty, beauty, grace and love. Their lengthy migratory flights make them symbols of strength and endurance.

THE CRANE FESTIVAL

Almost every village in Bhutan has religious festivals dedicated to local heroes and deities, as well as to the master teacher, Guru Rinpoche, who brought Buddhism from Tibet to Bhutan in the 8th century. In the Phobjika Valley, festivals are held at the Gangtey Monastery where prayers, songs, and both traditional and religious dances are performed.

The Crane Festival is held every year on November 11th. First initiated by the Royal Society for the Protection of Nature in 1998, it is now organized by the Phobjika Environment Management Committee along with support from the International Crane Foundation, the RSPN and others. The popularity of the Crane Festival provides an additional source of income to some farmers in the Valley who now can also benefit from eco-tourism.

Bhutanese festivals include dances that have been performed the same way for hundreds of years. The Crane Festival, however, is a "modern" creation that combines traditional dances—mostly performed by monks—with new dances performed by school children. The Crane Festival is the first and only festival in Bhutan dedicated to environmental education, telling the story that cranes and humans can co-exist.

COUNTING CRANES

Counting each individual bird is a challenge, but it provides valuable information for scientists and researchers concerned about crane conservation. Changes in crane populations may indicate loss of habitat, shifts in pollution levels, migration timing, climate change and more.

A flock of 200 to 300 black-necked cranes flies down from Tibet to spend the winter in the Phobjika Valley where Kinga—also known as Crane Boy—lives in our story. These graceful, elegant birds are some of the 5,000 black-necked cranes left in the world today. The cranes' survival will depend on the continued collective action of scientists, farmers, conservationists, monks, teachers, students and others, including you—the readers of this book. To learn more about how you can help, please visit www.savingcranes.org and www.rspnbhutan.org

TASHI DELEK!
Blessings—and may many good things come to you!

ACKNOWLEDGMENTS

WE RESPECTFULLY ACKNOWLEDGE His Majesty Jigme Singye Wangchuck, 4th Druk Gyalpo of Bhutan, and His Majesty Jigme Khesar Namgyel Wangchuck, 5th Druk Gyalpo of Bhutan, for their vision for environmental conservation and Gross National Happiness—a model for human and nature-centered economic development. We also respectfully acknowledge Her Majesty Queen Jetsun Pema Wangchuck, the Royal Patroness of the Royal Society for Protection of Nature, for her leadership and guidance in environmental conservation.

OUR HEARTFELT THANKS to our guide & mentor Kesang Dorji, who organized our research meetings and focus groups and participated in every aspect of developing *Crane Boy* while we were in Bhutan and our driver Penjor who made our trip safe and welcomed us into his family's home.

A VERY SPECIAL KAADINCHHEY LA (THANK YOU) to the dedicated ecologists, "craniacs," and caretakers of the earth in Bhutan from the Royal Society for Protection of Nature (including Ugyen Rinzin, Dr. Kinley Tenzin, Tshering Phuntsho, Lam Dorji and Jigme Tshering), and George Archibald, Richard Beilfuss, Dr. Li Fengshan and others from the International Crane Foundation for their feedback and support of *Crane Boy*, as well as to birdwatcher extraordinaire Hishey Tshering, Karma Lotey, CEO Yangphel Travel, and Mike McClelland of the Bhutan Friendship Foundation.

A DEEP BOW OF GRATITUDE to Lam Sangay, head of education at the Gangtey Goempa for his blessings and feedback and to Lama Dorji at the Gangtey Shedra.

A BOWL OF DELICIOUS EMA DATSE (CHILIS AND CHEESE) for Dechen Dema and the other teachers, administrators and students at the Bayta Primary School who welcomed us to their classrooms. To Pemba for showing us the crane dance steps and inviting us into his home. To all the children who listened to Crane Boy, asked us questions and made beautiful drawings of the cranes.

WE GIVE OUR THANKS to those who supported the creation of this book including Lee and Bobby Byrd, Johnny Byrd, Mary Fountaine and Anne Giangiulio of Cinco Puntos Press, Michele Coffey and Ann Delaney of the Lambent Foundation, and Scott Treimel, Barbara Young, Holly Payne, Ann Dowley, Jennifer Beckman, Lisa Schubert, Brenda Murad, Annika Merrilees, Amy Goodman, May Liang, Patricia Wefald, Lisl Schoepflin, Cheri Forrester, Robin Terra, Janet Shenk, Leslie and Jacques Leslie, Nikos Valance, Zoe Lane, Marion Hunt, Alison Merrilees, Karen Greenspan, Margaret Diehl, Margrit Elliot, and Phyllis Bergman & Richard Berg. Thanks to Matt Kirkpatrick for his origami cranes.

AND A SPECIAL BOW OF GRATITUDE to both our families—all dedicated caretakers of the earth—Barbara and Bert Cohn, Craig Merrilees, Hai Nguyen Ly, Edith, David and Mahayana Landowne, and Song and Tao, for their daily encouragement and belief in this book. And finally our deepest thanks to all the generous individuals (too numerous to mention) who contributed to our Books for Bhutan Campaign especially Ron Rankin, Hans Schoepflin, Thubten Losel Dawa, and Dr. Charles J. Betlach II and the Betlach Family Foundation who made it possible for copies of *Crane Boy* to be distributed to schools and libraries throughout Bhutan.

Library of Congress Cataloging-in-Publication Data
Cohn, Diana. Crane Boy / by Diana Cohn ; illustrated by Youme. — First edition. pages cm. Summary: Every year Kinga waits for the black-necked cranes to return to the kingdom of Bhutan, deep in the Himalayas. When he learns they are endangered, he wants to find a way to help. Kinga and his classmates create and perform a dance to honor the cranes and to remind people to protect them.— Provided by publisher. ISBN 978-1-941026-17-5 (pbk. : alk. paper); ISBN 978-1-941026-16-8 (hardback : alk. paper); ISBN 978-1-941026-18-2 (eBook) [1. Black-necked crane—Fiction. 2. Cranes (Birds)—Fiction. 3. Wildlife conservation—Fiction. 4. Dance—Fiction. 5. Festivals—Fiction. 6. Bhutan—Fiction.] I. Youme, illustrator. II. Title. PZ7.C6649Cr 2015   [E]—dc23 2014032020

Crane photos by Nick Bray / Zoothera Birding; photo of Youme and Diana by Kesang Dorji; photo of yak by Paul Allen Photography; photo of red panda by Greg Hume. All other photos are by Diana Cohn.

Book design by Anne M. Giangiulio